DRAGON MASTERS
COLLECTION

THREE BOOKS IN ONE!

BY

TRACEY WEST

BRANCHES

SCHOLASTIC INC.

ISBN 978-1-338-30586-9

10 9 8 7 6 5 4 3 2   20 21 22

Printed in the U.S.A.   23
First printing 2018
Illustrated by Graham Howells and Damien Jones
Edited by Katie Carella
Book design by Jessica Meltzer

DRAGON MASTERS
COLLECTION

TABLE OF CONTENTS

Book 1: Rise of the Earth Dragon 1

Book 2: Saving the Sun Dragon 95

Book 3: Secret of the Water Dragon 189

DRAGON MASTERS

RISE OF THE EARTH DRAGON

TRACEY
WEST

■SCHOLASTIC

TABLE OF CONTENTS

1. TO THE CASTLE! 3

2. THE DRAGON STONE 10

3. MORE DRAGONS! 17

4. WORM 21

5. DO SOMETHING! 26

6. A NEW FRIEND 32

7. A STRANGE DREAM 37

8. FLYING PRACTICE 43

9. WHISPERS 51

10. WORM'S STORY 56

11. A NOISE IN THE NIGHT 63

12. A SNEAKY PLAN 67

13. TROUBLE IN THE TUNNEL 73

14. TRAPPED! 77

15. WORM'S SURPRISE 83

16. JUST THE BEGINNING 87

CHAPTER 1

TO THE CASTLE!

Drake didn't see the king's soldier coming. He was busy digging in the onion patch. He pulled out a fat, white onion. A worm crawled on it. Drake didn't mind the worm. He was the son of a farmer. His family had been growing onions in the Kingdom of Bracken forever. He would spend his life digging up onions, whether he wanted to or not.

Drake picked up the worm.

"Hello, little guy," he said. Then he put the worm back in the dirt.

"Are you Drake?" a loud voice asked behind him.

Drake jumped and turned around. One of the king's soldiers rode up on a black horse. He had a yellow beard. His shirt had a gold dragon sewn on it — the symbol of King Roland the Bold.

"Yes, I'm Drake," Drake said, his voice shaking. Soldiers never came to the fields. Not unless a farmer was in trouble.

The soldier rode up to Drake. He reached down and pulled him up onto his horse.

"Hey, what are you doing?" Drake yelled. The soldier didn't answer.

Drake's mother ran out of their hut.

"Wait! Where are you taking my boy?" she yelled.

"To King Roland," the soldier said.

Drake's heart jumped a little. He had always wanted to meet the king.

"But he's only eight!" his mother yelled. She marched up to the horse.

"The king has chosen him," the soldier said.

Chosen me for what? Drake wondered. He knew better than to ask the soldier questions. Peasants like Drake weren't allowed to speak unless spoken to.

"The king will take good care of him," the soldier said. Then he spurred on the horse, and sped off.

"Drake, do as the king says!" his mother called out.

Drake had never been on a horse before. He held on tight.

Drake's heart pumped fast as they raced through the village. They raced over the stone bridge. Finally, they stopped in front of King Roland's castle.

The soldier helped Drake climb down from the horse. He opened the castle door and gave Drake a shove. They passed paintings and statues and people in fancy clothes. The soldier stomped behind Drake as they walked through the halls. Drake wanted to look at everything, but the soldier gave him a push whenever he slowed down.

Then they came to some stairs. They walked down ... down ... down. The soldier stopped at a door.

"Where are we going?" Drake finally asked.

"We are not going anywhere," the soldier said. "Good luck." Then he ran back up the stairs.

"Hey! What do you mean?" Drake yelled. But he was all alone.

Drake looked at the big, stone door. He felt
afraid. But more than that, he was curious.
He pushed it open and saw . . .

. . . the face of a giant, red
dragon!

Drake blinked. He didn't
believe his *eyes*. Then—
whoosh! — the dragon shot
a huge fireball from his mouth!

THE DRAGON STONE

rake dove away from the door. The fireball just missed him!

"Vulcan, stand down!" he heard someone yell.

Drake stood up. A red-haired girl was standing in the doorway.

"No more fireballs!" she yelled at the dragon. He had shiny red scales and a long, thick tail. Two big wings grew out of his back.

Dragons aren't real, thought Drake. But Drake could see the dragon. And he had felt the heat from the fireball.

A tall man walked past the girl. He had a long, white beard. He wore a pointy hat and a dark green robe.

"Welcome, Drake," the man said. "I am Griffith, the king's wizard."

Did he say "wizard"? Drake had so many questions! "Is that a dragon?" he asked.

"He's not just *a* dragon," said the girl. "He's *my* dragon. Vulcan is the *best* dragon in the kingdom."

"Drake, meet Rori," Griffith said. "Rori, please take Vulcan away. Tell the others I will be there shortly."

Others? Drake thought.

The girl sighed. "Fine. Let's go, Vulcan." She led the dragon away.

Then the wizard led Drake down a dark hall.

"Why am I here, sir?" Drake asked.

Griffith didn't answer. He stopped in front of a door. Griffith pointed at its big, brass lock. Sparks flew from his finger. The lock opened.

Drake's eyes grew wide. *Wizard magic!* he thought.

He followed Griffith into a room piled high with strange things. He saw bottles filled with colorful waters and powders.

Griffith picked up a wooden box. The box was carved with pictures of dragons.

"This is why you are here," he said, opening the box.

Drake peered inside. A green stone as big as his head glittered in the light.

"This Dragon Stone told me you have the heart of a dragon," said the wizard. He tapped Drake's chest.

"It d-did?" Drake asked. His eyes got big.

"Yes. And those with the heart of a dragon become Dragon Masters for King Roland," Griffith said.

Drake had heard stories about the magical Dragon Stone. But he had never believed they were real. Now all his questions came spilling out.

"How does the stone *know* I have the heart of a dragon? And how did you find me? And what's a Dragon Master? And why does King Roland want Dragon Masters?"

"The stone is old and mysterious," Griffith said. "Even I do not fully understand its magic. A Dragon Master is able to connect with dragons. As for the king . . . he is very fond of dragons. But he cannot control them."

"So Vulcan isn't the only dragon?" Drake asked.

The wizard grinned. "No, he is not."

He handed Drake a green stone on a gold chain. "This is a piece of the Dragon Stone," he said. "It will help you connect with your dragon."

Drake's heart jumped. *My dragon? I get a dragon?* he thought. He slipped the stone into his pocket.

"Be careful, Drake," the wizard warned. "Dragons are dangerous. And even the Dragon Stone can't protect you from their powers."

"What powers?" Drake asked.

The wizard led him away without another word.

MORE DRAGONS!

rake's mind was spinning as he left the
wizard's workshop. He followed Griffith
to a big underground room. There were no
windows. Torches hung on the walls. Drake
saw Rori and Vulcan. He also saw two more
kids — and two more dragons!

"Drake, this is Bo," Griffith said, pointing to a boy with black hair, "and his dragon, Shu."

Bo was petting his dragon's tail. This dragon had shiny blue scales, but no wings.

"Hi," Drake said.

"Nice to meet you, Drake," the boy said politely.

Griffith led Drake over to a girl with long, black hair. Her dragon had white scales. A yellow band of scales circled the dragon's neck. The tips of its wings were yellow, too.

"This is Ana, and her dragon, Kepri," Griffith said.

Drake nodded. "Hi," he said.

"We could use somebody new around here," Ana said with a grin.

"You have met the other Dragon Masters and their dragons. It is time for you to meet *your* dragon," Griffith said.

Drake's heart pounded. *My family will never believe this!* he thought. *Just this morning I was digging onions. Now I have ridden a horse. I've met a wizard. I've seen the Dragon Stone. And I'm going to have my very own dragon?!*

He and the other Dragon Masters followed Griffith down another dark hallway.

"The dragons sleep in caves when they're not training," Bo explained as they walked.

"Vulcan's cave is the biggest," bragged Rori.

Griffith stopped in front of a small cave. Wood bars covered the cave.

"Drake, meet your dragon!" the wizard said.

WORM

Drake peered inside the dark cave. A dragon sat inside. *Well, this creature kind of looks like a dragon*, Drake thought. The dragon had brown scales that weren't shiny. He had two tiny wings. He had big, green eyes, and little ears. And he didn't have legs! He looked like a big snake.

The only dragon-like thing about him seemed to be his long snout.

CHAPTER 4

Drake stepped up to the wood bars. "Hi, dragon. I'm Drake."

The dragon didn't move.

"Put on the stone," Griffith said.

Drake slipped the green stone around his neck. He felt a tingly feeling all over his body.

Right away, the dragon lifted his head. He stared at Drake with his big, green eyes. Drake felt a strange chill.

Griffith stepped forward. "You must name your dragon," he said.

Rori piped up. "Good luck naming *him*. He looks boring."

"How about Noodle Head?" Ana asked with a giggle.

Bo shook his head. "No, this dragon needs a good name."

Drake looked carefully at the dragon. He looked at his long, brown body.

"Worm," he said. "His name is Worm."

"That is a good name for an Earth Dragon," said Griffith, opening the gate. "Now, Drake, ask Worm to follow you."

"Okay," Drake said. "Worm, please follow me."

Worm crawled forward.

"Good work!" said the wizard. "Keep it up, Drake."

"Come on," Drake said, starting to walk down the hallway. Worm crawled after him.

"He really is like a big, ugly worm," Rori said.

"Rori, be nice," said Ana.

Drake didn't say anything. Worm *was* like a big worm.

"Where are we going?" he asked.

"To the Training Room," Griffith replied.

"Yeah," said Rori. "We'll see what you and your dragon are made of."

Drake felt nervous. He touched his Dragon Stone. *How am I supposed to train a dragon?* he thought. *What if I fail? What if I'm not a Dragon Master after all?*

CHAPTER 5

DO SOMETHING!

The Training Room was one big, open space. Shields and long poles hung from the walls. Buckets held water and sand. And at one end of the room was a round target. Straw stuffing poked out from the sides.

Griffith pointed at the target. Sparks flew from his finger and a red bull's-eye showed up on the target.

"It's time for target practice!" the wizard said.

"Me first!" Rori called out. "Vulcan, come!"

The red dragon stomped forward.

"Vulcan, fire!" Rori yelled.

The dragon's orange eyes glowed. Then two streams of fire shot from his nose. The streams twisted together. The fire hit the bull's-eye.

"Perfect!" Rori cheered.

Then the straw burst into flames!

Drake jumped back.

"Good aim," said Griffith. "Bo, can you help put the fire out?"

"Yes," said Bo. He looked at his dragon.

"Shu," he said simply. He didn't yell like Rori.

Shu swiftly crossed the room. *Did her feet even touch the ground?* wondered Drake.

"Water, please, Shu," Bo said.

A stream of water sprayed out of the blue dragon's mouth.

The fire sizzled. Water droplets danced in the air, lit up by the torches.

"Kepri! Rainbow time!" Ana cried.

Kepri glided across the room. Drake thought her white scales looked like jewels.

A soft beam of light came out of Kepri's mouth. It grew wider and wider. When it hit the water droplets, it made a rainbow!

"Wow," Drake said.

"Isn't she amazing?" asked Bo.

Ana smiled.

Rori put her hands on her hips.

"Now let's see what Worm can do," she said.

Drake felt nervous. He looked at Worm.

"Um, Worm, are you ready?" Drake asked.

Worm stared back at him.

I guess that means yes, thought Drake. "Okay, Worm. Fire!"

Drake jumped back in case fire came out of Worm's mouth. But Worm just lay there.

"Not all dragons can shoot fire," said Bo.

Drake nodded. "Right. Okay, Worm. Water!"

But Worm didn't shoot water.

"Ha!" Rori laughed. "I knew it. Worm can't do anything."

Drake's cheeks grew hot with anger. "He's just warming up," he said. "Come on, Worm. Shoot light out of your mouth!"

Still nothing.

"You call that a dragon?" Rori said.

"Please, Worm?" Drake whispered to his dragon. "Do something!"

Worm just blinked.

"Do not worry, Drake. Getting to know your dragon takes time," Griffith said. "Target practice is over for today. Let's go eat."

Bo grabbed Drake's elbow.

"I hope you're hungry, Drake! The Dragon Masters get as much food as we want," said Bo.

Drake was hungry so this news made him feel a little better. But he had failed the training. *How can I be a Dragon Master if my dragon won't do anything I ask it to do?* he thought. *I'm only an onion farmer. I don't belong here.*

CHAPTER 6

A NEW FRIEND

There was so much food on the dining room table! Roast chicken. Potatoes. Carrots. Bread. Cheese. It was more food than Drake had seen in his life.

"Pass the potatoes, please," Drake said.

Griffith pointed to the plate of potatoes. Sparks flew from his finger.

As the plate floated over to Drake, he forgot all about wanting to go home. He stabbed a potato with his fork.

"Is every supper like this?" Drake asked Bo.

Bo nodded. "Yes, there is always a great deal of good food," he said. "But sometimes I miss my mother's soup."

"Is your home kingdom far away?" Drake asked.

"Very far," said Bo. "I come from the east — the kingdom of Emperor Song."

"And I come from the south," added Ana. "It is warm there. Not cold and damp like it is here."

"Well, I am proud to be from *this* kingdom," Rori said. "My father is a blacksmith. He makes the best horseshoes in our village."

Drake missed home. He turned to Griffith.

"Is there a way I can let my family know I'm okay?" Drake asked.

The wizard nodded. "You may send them a note." He waved to one of the servants. "Please bring this boy paper and a quill."

A servant gave Drake paper, a small pot of ink, and a feather. Drake's cheeks turned red.

"What?" Rori asked. "Haven't you seen paper before?"

Drake looked down at his plate. "I worked in the fields at home," he said. "I never went to school. I know how to read. But we never had paper. Or quills. So I don't know how to write."

Rori started to say something, but Griffith gave her a hard look. Bo picked up the quill.

"I will write the note for you," he said.

"Thanks," Drake said. Then he told Bo what to write.

Dear Mother,

I am safe so please do not worry. Everything is new and exciting. The king is keeping me well fed. My new friend Bo helped me write this letter.

Love,
Drake

Drake did not say anything about dragons. He thought that might scare his mother.

The servant took the note away.

Drake yawned. "So, where do we sleep?"

"We have rooms in the tower," Bo said. "You will be in my room."

Drake smiled. "Good." At least he had one new friend here.

Suddenly, a soldier stomped into the room.

"All rise for King Roland the Bold!" he said.

CHAPTER 7

A STRANGE DREAM

The Dragon Masters jumped to their feet. King Roland swept into the room. He was a big man, with red hair and a bushy beard. He walked right up to Drake. Drake was so nervous, he was shaking.

"*This* is my new Dragon Master?" he asked.

"Yes, Your Highness," said Griffith.

The king frowned. "He's scrawny."

Drake felt like sinking into the floor.

The king turned to Griffith. "Explain this to me, wizard. My strongest men cannot control dragons. Why is it that these children can?"

"It is the way of the Dragon Stone," Griffith said. "It is a mystery, even to me."

"*Hmph!*" snorted the king. "Very well, then. I shall leave my army in your hands."

Army? Drake wondered.

King Roland looked at Drake again.

"Do not let me down, boy," he said. Then he and the soldier left. Everyone sat back down.

The king's words scared Drake. *What will happen if I do let him down?* Drake wondered. He had a feeling it wouldn't be good.

Bo took Drake to their room. There was a bed and a wooden chest for each of them. There was also a desk for them to share. A jug of water sat on a table.

"That is your bed," Bo said, pointing.

Drake climbed into bed.

The moon shone through a small window. Drake looked over at Bo. He was already sleeping peacefully. Drake soon drifted off to sleep, too.

All of a sudden, he was in a dark cave.

The air in the cave felt warm. It smelled like the deep, rich dirt where the onions grew. Green eyes glowed in the darkness.

Worm! Worm was in the cave. And behind him were other dragons. They all had the same brown scales and green eyes.

Boom! A loud explosion shook the cave. Smoke filled the air. Worm let out a cry. The dragons slithered across the cave floor, looking for a way out.

Drake woke up in his bed, dripping sweat. *That was some nightmare,* he thought. *It felt so real. . . .*

FLYING PRACTICE

After breakfast the next morning, Drake went back underground with Griffith and the other Dragon Masters.

"Why do we train all the way down here?" Drake asked as they walked.

"Don't you know?" Rori said. "We're a *secret*. No one knows the dragons are here. No one knows the Dragon Stone is real. And no one knows about us."

Drake looked at the wizard.

"It is true," Griffith said. "The king does not want others to know about the dragons."

"Because he's building a dragon army?" Drake asked.

"That is the king's business, not ours," said Griffith. He opened the door to the hallway of dragon caves. "Collect your dragons. We are going outside today."

"Hooray!" yelled Ana, Rori, and Bo.

"But won't someone see us if we go outside?" asked Drake.

"No, we'll be hidden in the Valley of Clouds," said Ana. "Hurry, go get Worm!"

Drake ran through the winding hallway to Worm's cave. Worm raised his head and looked at him. It reminded Drake of his nightmare. He shivered.

"Come on, Worm. We are going outside," Drake said, as he opened the gate.

Worm crawled out of his cave.

Griffith led them all down a dark tunnel.

The tunnel opened up into a bright field of grass. Tall hills rose up on all sides.

"The sun!" cheered Ana. She twirled around.

Drake looked up at the sun and smiled.

"So what do we do out here?" he asked.

Ana grinned. "We fly," she said. She patted Kepri on the head. "Show him, girl."

Kepri raised her long neck and flew straight up. She looped and swirled in the air. Drake watched her, shading his eyes from the sun. He had never seen anything like it.

"Wait till you see Vulcan fly," Rori said. "Vulcan! Circle!"

Vulcan flapped his big, red wings. He flew up into the sky and circled the field.

"Wow!" Drake said.

He looked over at Bo.

"Your dragon doesn't have wings, but can she fly, too?" he asked.

Bo nodded. "She does not need wings," he said. "Shu, please fly." Shu floated up off the grass.

"It's like she's swimming through the air," Drake said.

"Yes," said Bo. "How Shu flies is very much like how one swims. She can ride the winds."

Drake looked at Worm. His tiny wings did not look like they could lift him. "What about you, Worm?" he asked. "Can you fly, too?"

Worm just stared at Drake. He didn't flap his wings. He didn't even move.

"It's okay," Drake said. He thought of how scared Worm had been in the nightmare. "We can watch the others."

Drake sat on the grass. He put a hand on Worm's back. The dragon moved a little closer to him.

Suddenly, the Dragon Stone felt warm on Drake's skin. He looked down. It was glowing! Drake looked around. Griffith was standing over with the other Dragon Masters. None of their stones were glowing.

Why is my stone glowing? he wondered. *Am I doing something wrong?*

Drake quickly tucked his Dragon Stone
inside his shirt. Then he went back to watching
the other dragons fly across the sky.

WHISPERS

And that is how to shine a dragon's scales,"
Griffith was saying later that week. "Remember,
brush one scale at a time. No shortcuts."

Rori sighed. "When can we go out again?"

Drake was glad Rori had asked. They had
been stuck in the Training Room for three days.

Drake liked learning about dragons, but he was used to being outside all day every day on his farm back home. He was starting to forget what the sun looked like.

The wizard patted a tall pile of books on his desk. "There is much for you to learn first. We will go out again soon, Rori."

Then a soldier came in. He handed something to Griffith.

The wizard smiled. "Drake, it is a letter for you."

"Read it out loud!" Ana said.

Drake quickly nodded to Griffith.

Dear Drake,
     We are glad you are safe. We still don't know why the king brought you there. Can you tell us?

Please keep writing so we won't worry. And thank you to your friend Bo for helping you to write to us.
          Love,
          Your Mother

"Your mother sounds nice," Bo said.

Drake's eyes started to burn. He held back his tears. "Thanks," he said. "May I send another letter to tell her about the dragons?"

"You must not say anything about the dragons," Griffith said. "The king's secret must be kept."

The wizard stood up. "Now, it is time to shine your dragons. Let us go."

As they were leaving the Training Room, Rori ran over to Ana. She started whispering to her.

Drake kept an eye on Rori as they walked toward the dragon caves. *She has a sneaky look on her face,* he thought. *What are she and Ana up to?*

CHAPTER 10

WORM'S STORY

Drake stepped inside Worm's dark cave. Worm opened one eye.

"I need to shine your scales," Drake said. He was carrying a brush, a basket, and towels.

Drake looked at Worm's brown scales. "They're not shiny," he said. "But I'll clean them anyway."

Drake was still getting used to being around Worm. The dragon's head was as big as Drake. Worm could swallow Drake in one gulp if he wanted to. But something about Worm made Drake feel . . . peaceful.

Drake gently brushed one of Worm's scales. The big dragon made a sound low in his throat. Worm smiled and closed his eyes.

"You like that?" Drake asked. Worm made another purring sound. "Good."

He cleaned Worm's scales, one at a time.

"I kind of miss the onion field back home," Drake said to his dragon. "It was hard work. But I loved being outside."

Drake started to clean Worm's head.

"And I really miss my family," Drake said.

He scratched behind Worm's ears, like he did with his cat back home. Then he felt his hand start tingling. . . . He tried to take his hand off Worm, but he couldn't. It was stuck. Drake's eyes widened. He looked at Worm. The dragon was staring hard at him.

Pictures popped into Drake's head. He saw the cave from his nightmare. He saw the explosion again. Before, Drake had woken up. This time, the pictures kept coming. . . .

Worm was trying to get out of the cave, but the other dragons were in the way. Then soldiers rushed into the cave. Each soldier's shirt had a gold dragon sewn on it.

"The king's soldiers?" Drake asked.

The soldiers wrapped Worm in chains. They dragged him out of the cave. *Owwwreeeeee!* Drake could hear Worm's cry. Then his hand stopped tingling. The pictures left his head.

Drake looked at Worm. "Did that really happen? Did the king's men take you away from your family? Just like they took me away from mine?"

Worm nodded.

"I'm so sorry," Drake said. He threw his arms around Worm's neck. Worm closed his eyes.

All his life, Drake had looked up to King Roland. *But why would the king's men treat Worm like a prisoner?* wondered Drake. *Maybe he isn't such a good king after all.*

CHAPTER 11

A NOISE IN THE NIGHT

"Good job cleaning Worm's scales, Drake," Griffith said, walking into the cave.

Drake wasn't going to say anything about what Worm had shown him. Not yet. But he did have a question for Griffith.

"How did the dragons get here?" he asked.

"The king's soldiers searched far and wide," Griffith replied. "It is not easy to find a dragon. Most people have never seen one. But the king did not give up. His soldiers were able to capture these four."

"But did the dragons *want* to come here?" Drake asked.

"The king does not always think about what dragons want," Griffith said darkly. "Now come. It is time for supper."

After they ate, Bo and Drake went to their room. Bo was teaching him how to write the alphabet.

Bo drew a capital *D* and a lowercase *d*.

"See?" Bo said. "The big *D* looks like a dragon with a big belly." He drew a picture on the paper.

"Like Vulcan," Drake said with a laugh. Bo laughed, too.

Moonlight glinted off Bo's Dragon Stone. It reminded Drake of something he'd wanted to ask Bo about.

"Does your stone ever glow?" Drake asked.

Bo shook his head. "No," he said. "Why do you ask?"

"It's just . . . I thought I saw mine glow once," Drake said. "When I was with Worm."

"That's interesting," Bo said. "You should tell Griffith."

Drake nodded. "Tomorrow," he said.

Drake wrote rows of the letter *D* before he went to sleep. He thought he would dream of *D*s — or maybe of Worm again. But just after he climbed into bed . . .

Thunk! Drake heard a loud noise. He sat up and saw two figures standing by Bo's bed!

A SNEAKY PLAN

he two figures turned around. It was Rori and Ana!

"What do *you* want?" Drake asked.

"Go back to sleep," Rori snapped.

"Why should I?" he snapped back. Drake was tired of Rori being so bossy.

"Yeah, why should he?" Bo said. "And why are you two here?"

Ana spoke up. "We are going to bring our dragons outside while the rest of the castle is asleep. Do you guys want to come? You can bring Worm and Shu."

"This is a bad idea," Bo said.

"No, it's not!" Rori said. "We're Dragon Masters! We should be able to take our dragons out whenever we want to."

"You have a point," Drake agreed. "And I do think Worm would like to go outside again."

Bo looked worried. "What if Griffith finds out?" he asked. "What if *the king* finds out?"

"They won't find out," Rori said. "So long as neither of you say anything." She looked them both in the eyes.

"Well, come on, then!" said Ana.

Drake slipped on his shoes. He followed the others down the hall. The door to Griffith's room was open. He was snoring loudly.

ZZZZzzzzzzzzzzzzzz!

Rori put a finger to her lips. *"Shhh!"*

As they tiptoed past the door, Drake peeked inside. The wizard's long beard flew up every time he snored.

The Dragon Masters walked down the stairs. The guard in front of the Training Room door was asleep, too.

"That's Simon," Rori whispered. "He always falls asleep."

They tiptoed past Simon and into the Training Room. The torches were not lit, so the room was black. Rori lit a candle. Then she passed candles to each of them.

"Now, let's get the dragons!" she said, still whispering.

They reached Vulcan's cave first. Rori opened the gate.

"Wake up, Vulcan," she said. "We're going outside."

Grumbling, Vulcan got to his feet. Ana and Bo woke up their dragons. Drake went into Worm's cave.

"Worm, do you want to go outside?" Drake asked.

Worm lifted his head. His eyes shot wide open. They stared right at Drake. Drake got a strange feeling.

"Come on, Worm," Drake said.

But Worm didn't move. He just stared at Drake. *Is he trying to tell me something?* Drake wondered.

Rori, Ana, and Bo walked up to Worm's cave with their dragons.

"Is Worm coming?" Rori asked.

Suddenly, Drake froze. He heard words inside his head: *Do not go into the tunnel!*

TROUBLE IN THE TUNNEL

id Worm just speak to me . . . through his thoughts? Drake did not know what to think. But he had a feeling those words of warning had come from Worm.

"Drake, what's the matter?" Ana asked.

"It's . . . I'm not sure," he said. *What would they think if I told them I just heard words in my head?* "Worm doesn't want to go."

"Fine. Stay here. Be a big chicken," Rori snapped.

"I didn't say I was staying," Drake shot back. "I'll come along without Worm."

As soon as he said it, Worm crawled out of the cave.

"Look! He is coming with us!" Ana said.

Drake didn't hear any more words in his head. Maybe Worm had changed his mind.

Rori led Vulcan forward. "Let's get moving."

They headed into the long tunnel that led outside. The torches on the walls weren't lit. And their candles weren't doing much to light things up.

"Kepri can light the way," Ana said. But before she could give the command, Rori cried out, "Look!"

Drake craned his neck to look around the dragons in front of him. Then he saw it. A glowing, red orb floated toward them. It grew bigger and bigger as it got closer.

"That looks like wizard's magic!" Ana cried.

"But it is not Griffith's magic," said Bo. "It feels . . . scary."

Just then, Vulcan let out a loud roar. His big tail thrashed back and forth.

"Calm down, Vulcan!" Rori yelled. But her dragon was very upset.

Whack! Whack! Vulcan's tail banged against
the sides of the tunnel. His big body slammed
against the walls. Kepri and Shu cried out.
They both tried to turn back. Only Worm
stayed calm.

The tunnel began to shake. Dirt fell from
the walls. The Dragon Masters all looked at
one another.

"Run!" Drake yelled, but it was too late.

The walls caved in around them!

TRAPPED!

Drake ducked as dirt rained down. He closed his eyes tight.

Then the shaking stopped. Drake opened his eyes.

All the candles had gone out. He looked behind him in the darkness. "Worm, are you all right?"

Worm looked fine. In fact, he didn't have any dust on him. Everybody else was pretty dirty.

"Is everybody okay?" Drake asked.

Ana was on the ground. Bo helped her up. "I'm fine," she said. "That was scary, though!"

Rori walked over. "I'm sorry," she said. "I don't know why that weird ball of light made Vulcan freak out."

Drake looked around. "Thankfully, it's gone now."

"We should get back," Bo said nervously.

Drake looked past Worm. The tunnel was blocked with rocks and dirt.

"I don't think we can," Drake said.

"The way outside is blocked, too," Rori said.

"We're trapped!" said Bo. He turned pale.

Ana's dragon made a sad sound.

"It's okay, Kepri," Ana said, stroking Kepri's snout. "Can you give us some light, please?"

Kepri opened her mouth and a beautiful, white ball of light came out. The light hung in the air.

"Vulcan is strong," Rori said. "He should be able to push through the rocks."

Vulcan was calmer now that the red orb was gone. He pushed at the rock wall, but the rocks didn't budge.

"Come on, Vulcan!" Rori urged him. But Vulcan couldn't break through.

Bo spoke up. "I could have Shu blast through the rocks with water."

Ana frowned. "What if it doesn't work? Then the tunnel will fill with water."

Everybody was quiet. They knew Ana was right. They were stuck.

Drake looked at Worm. "Sorry I got you into this," he whispered.

Then Worm's green eyes started to glow.
A green light swept from the top of Worm's
head to the end of his tail.

Drake jumped back. "Worm?" He felt something warm on his chest. He looked down to see that his Dragon Stone was glowing, too!

Ana, Rori, and Bo's mouths dropped open. They stared at Worm and Drake. Worm's green glow filled the tunnel.

"Drake, it looks like your dragon's going to explode!" Rori yelled.

WORM'S SURPRISE

Worm didn't explode. Instead, the dragon closed his eyes.

Then the rocks blocking the tunnel began to shake.

"What's happening?!" Bo yelled.

"Is Worm doing that?" asked Ana.

"I think . . . I think he's using the power of his mind," Drake said. He wasn't sure how he knew. He just did.

Rori, Ana, and Bo stepped back. The rocks kept shaking. Then . . .

Poof! The rocks broke up into tiny pieces. Rock dust filled the air. Drake coughed, waving the dust away with his hand. All of the fallen rocks were gone. The tunnel was clear again!

Drake hugged Worm. "You did it, Worm!"

"We should get out of here before Vulcan sneezes from all this dust," said Rori. "The last time he sneezed he turned my bread into toast."

"Rori's right," said Bo. "Let's get out of here."

Drake stepped through the pile of rubble —
and found himself face-to-face with Griffith.
Simon the guard stood behind Griffith.

"You are all in *big* trouble!" the wizard said.
"The whole castle is awake. And King Roland
is furious!"

JUST THE BEGINNING

The group walked back through the tunnel in silence. Six of the king's guards were waiting for them in the Training Room. One stepped forward as soon as they entered the room.

"King Roland wants a report!" he barked.

The Dragon Masters all looked to Griffith.

He cleared his throat. "Please tell King Roland that everything is fine," he said. "The dragons tried to escape. But the Dragon Masters stopped them."

"But —" Drake started to speak, but something about Griffith's look told him to stay quiet.

The soldier nodded to Griffith. "Very well," he said. Then the soldiers and Simon left.

Drake turned to Griffith. "But the dragons didn't do anything wrong," he said.

Rori stepped forward. "Drake's right. This was my fault. I wanted to take the dragons outside," she said. She turned to the Dragon Masters. "I'm sorry. It was a bad idea."

"Agreed," said Griffith. "Now tell me: How did you all get *out* of the collapsed tunnel?"

"Worm saved us!" Rori cried.

Ana nodded. "He glowed all green. It was amazing!"

"And he turned the rocks to dust!" Bo added.

The wizard's eyes lit up. "That's excellent!" He grabbed Drake by the shoulders. "I knew you could bring it out of him, Drake!"

"Earth Dragons have great power," Griffith said. "Worm has been hiding his power. Until now. He glowed because he was using it."

"Is that why my Dragon Stone glowed, too?" Drake asked.

"No. The stone glows when you have a strong link with your dragon," Griffith said. "The link is strong when you and your dragon can read each other's thoughts. It will happen to the other Dragon Masters, too, in time."

Drake remembered the words he had heard in his head.

"Thank you, Worm," he said, stroking him. "You really saved us today."

"Wait! We forgot to tell you about the red ball of light," Rori piped up. "That's what scared Vulcan. When it flew into the tunnel, he panicked and made the tunnel collapse."

A cloud came over Griffith's face. "Are you sure that you saw a *red* ball of light?"

All four Dragon Masters nodded.

"This is serious," Griffith said. "Danger may be heading our way."

"Danger?" Bo asked.

Griffith patted Bo's head. "For now, we are safe. Let's all get some sleep."

As Drake led Worm back to his cave, he felt a strong connection to his dragon. He wasn't going back to the onion fields. This was his life now — a life full of dragons and magic and danger.

He was a Dragon Master.

DRAGON MASTERS
RISE OF THE EARTH DRAGON

Questions and Activities

Look at the picture on top of page 12. How do you think Rori **FEELS** about Drake?

Why does Worm follow Drake through the tunnel even though he warned Drake not to go?

How does Worm **SAVE** the Dragon Masters?

Why do you think the Dragon Masters confess to Griffith that it was their idea to bring the dragons outside?

If you had a dragon, what kind of special power would you want it to have? **DRAW** a picture of your dragon performing the special power.

scholastic.com/branches

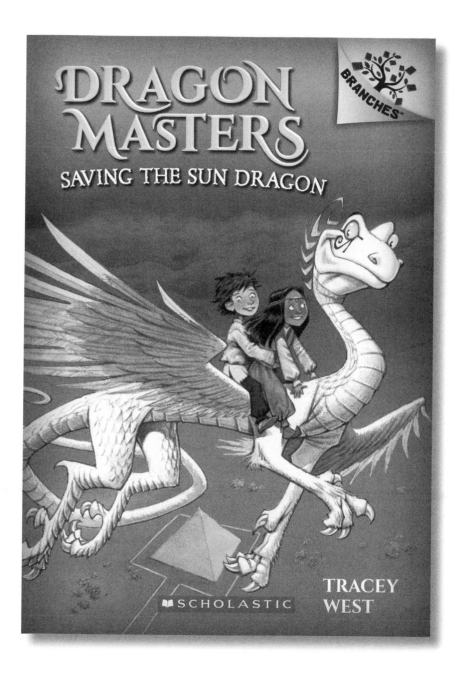

TABLE OF CONTENTS

1. DRAGONS IN THE SKY 97

2. A SICK DRAGON 106

3. KING ROLAND'S THREAT 115

4. THE WIZARD'S POTION 120

5. ANA'S STORY 129

6. WORM CALLS 137

7. FAR-AWAY LANDS 142

8. A STRANGE BOY 148

9. KEPRI AND WATI 153

10. ROBBERS! 159

11. FLYING 163

12. ANA'S DECISION 168

13. ONE LAST GOOD-BYE 174

14. HOME 178

DRAGONS IN THE SKY

Drake shaded his eyes from the sun. He was standing in the Valley of Clouds behind King Roland's castle. Not long ago, Drake had never even been to the castle. But now he lived here, and he had an important job. He was a Dragon Master—someone who had been chosen by the Dragon Stone to work with dragons.

Above him, three dragons flew in the bright blue sky. Griffith, the wizard who taught the young Dragon Masters, watched as the dragons practiced flying.

Vulcan, a big, red Fire Dragon, flew across
the valley. He shot a burst of fire into the air.

"Nice one!" yelled his Dragon Master, Rori.
She had hair as red as Vulcan's flames.

Shu, a beautiful blue Water Dragon, didn't
have wings. She glided through the air, riding
the wind. Bo, her Dragon Master, watched her
with a peaceful smile on his face.

The best flier was the yellow and white Sun
Dragon, Kepri. She looped and swirled in the
air. Then a rainbow streamed from her mouth.
It arced across the sky. Kepri's Dragon Master,
Ana, danced on the grass below her dragon.
Her long, black hair swayed behind her.

Drake's dragon, Worm, was not like the
other dragons. He was an Earth Dragon with a
long, brown body. He couldn't fly. But Drake
had just learned Worm could move things with
the power of his mind. *What other amazing
things can Worm do?* Drake wondered. He
knew he had even more to learn about his
dragon.

"It feels good to be outside, right, Worm?"
Drake asked. The green Dragon Stone around
Drake's neck tingled a bit. He smiled.

Each of the Dragon Masters wore a piece of the stone. It helped them connect with and train their dragons.

When the stone glowed, Drake knew that he and Worm had a very strong connection. Drake could sometimes hear Worm's voice inside his head when they were connecting. But the other Dragon Masters' stones had not glowed yet.

Drake looked back up at the sunny sky. Kepri's whole body shone with light.

Then Drake understood. "Oh, I get it. Kepri has light powers because she's a Sun Dragon, right?" Drake asked the other Dragon Masters.

Rori snorted. "Of course that's why. It's just like how Fire Dragons have fire powers, and Water Dragons have water powers."

Rori can be friendly sometimes, thought Drake. *And other times she's not friendly at all!*

His face turned red. "I'm still learning," he said. "I haven't been a Dragon Master as long as you."

Rori, Bo, and Ana had already been training for weeks when Drake got to the castle. He still felt like he had a lot of catching up to do. Above them, Vulcan swooped down from the sky, showing off and shooting another stream of fire. It hit the ground right next to Griffith, and the grass burst into flames. The wizard jumped to the side.

"Careful there, Vulcan!" Griffith called out. He pointed his finger at the fire. Water flowed from his fingertip, and the flames went out.

Drake's eyes grew wide. "I will never get tired of seeing wizard magic," he said to Bo, who was standing beside him. Bo nodded.

Drake looked over at Worm. The dragon's eyes glowed bright green.

That's strange, thought Drake. *His eyes glow when he's using his powers. What could he be using his powers on right now?*

Worm was staring up at the sky.

Drake followed his gaze. Worm was looking at Kepri high up in the air. Her white wings had stopped flapping. Worm must have sensed that she was in trouble.

"Watch out! Kepri is falling!" Drake yelled.

A SICK DRAGON

Ana looked up and started to scream. The other Dragon Masters also looked to the sky. Griffith pointed a finger at Kepri.

"I'll try to slow her down!" the wizard cried. Lightning sizzled from his finger. But before Griffith could use his magic, a red blur shot across the sky.

It was Vulcan, flying faster than Drake had
ever seen him fly before. He lunged for Kepri
and grabbed her with his front claws.

"Go, Vulcan!" Rori cheered.

Vulcan flew in a circle around the valley,
slowing down. Then he gently placed Kepri
in the grass.

Everyone ran to Kepri. The dragon's eyes were closed. Her breathing was loud and heavy. Ana stroked Kepri's head.

"Oh, Kepri, are you all right?" she asked, her voice shaking.

Griffith leaned over Kepri, frowning. "I'm afraid she doesn't look well," he said.

Ana turned to the wizard. "She has seemed a little off since last week—when the tunnel caved in. She gets tired easily. And sometimes her eyes look cloudy. I should have said something!"

Griffith put a hand on her shoulder. "It's not your fault, Ana," he said. "But are you sure Kepri only started looking sick *after* that night in the tunnel?"

Ana slowly nodded her head. "Yes. She was fine before then."

Drake, Bo, and Rori looked at one another. A week before, they had all tried to sneak out of the castle with their dragons. Since King Roland wanted to keep the dragons a secret, most dragon training had to take place underground. The Dragon Masters had only wanted to get outside to do some night flying.

Then a glowing red orb had flown into the tunnel that led to the valley.

The red ball of light scared Vulcan so he tried to get away.

His huge body banged into the tunnel walls, and he had made the tunnel cave in.

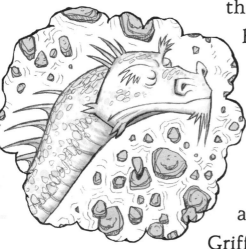

They were trapped.

Worm used his mind powers to help them escape. He broke up the big rocks blocking the tunnel using only his thoughts. Worm had saved them all.

But now something was wrong with Kepri.

"Why did you ask about the cave-in, Griffith?" asked Bo.

"The red orb worries me," Griffith answered. "It must have been made by a dark wizard, as I had feared. And dark magic can make Sun Dragons sick."

"So Kepri's illness is connected to that weird ball?" asked Ana. "And the other dragons are okay because they're *not* Sun Dragons?"

"I think so," said Griffith.

"Do you *know* any dark wizards?" Drake asked with a shiver.

"No time for tales now," said Griffith with a wave of his hand.

Suddenly, Rori cried out. "Look! Kepri is getting up!"

The dragon had opened her eyes and was standing on all four legs.

"She looks well enough to walk back to the dragon caves," Griffith said. "Come along."

He led the Dragon Masters and their dragons back through the tunnel. The tunnel led to the big, underground Dragon Room. There, each dragon had a small cave.

When they got there, a big man with red hair waited for them. He wore a vest with a gold dragon on it, and a metal crown on his head. Two guards stood behind him.

Griffith stopped. "King Roland!" he said. "What brings you down here?"

The king frowned. "What is this I hear about a sick dragon?"

KING ROLAND'S THREAT

Drake looked over at his friend Bo. He could tell Bo was thinking the same thing he was: *How did the king know one of the dragons was sick?*

"I have spies hidden in the Valley of Clouds," the king said, as if he had read their minds. "You almost let these dragons escape once, Griffith. I want to make sure they are ready when I need them."

"I understand," Griffith said.

Drake remembered that when the tunnel had caved in, Griffith hadn't told the king that the Dragon Masters had taken the dragons out. Instead, he said the dragons had tried to escape. Griffith had lied to protect the Dragon Masters.

Griffith had only wanted to protect us when he told that lie, Drake thought. *But now the king is mad at* him *instead of us!*

"So I will ask you again, Griffith," said the king. "Is one of the dragons sick?"

"Yes, Your Majesty," said Griffith. "There seems to be something wrong with Kepri."

All eyes turned to Kepri. Her eyes were cloudy. And her long, graceful neck was drooping.

"First the dragons tried to escape, and now one is sick," said King Roland. "This makes me very unhappy, wizard. You are supposed to know all about dragons. Heal her!"

"I will look for a cure right away," Griffith promised.

"You had better find one soon," King Roland said, his eyes fixed on the wizard. "If not, I will find another wizard."

King Roland turned and stormed out of the caves. His guards followed.

Drake's stomach did a flip. *Another wizard? What would we do without Griffith?*

"What do we do now?" Ana asked Griffith, stroking Kepri's head.

"I have many books about dragons," the wizard replied. "We will start there."

"We? You mean we can help?" Drake asked.

"Of course!" Griffith said. "Please take your dragons into their caves. Then meet me in the Training Room. We must act quickly to save Kepri!"

CHAPTER 4

THE WIZARD'S POTION

The Dragon Masters dropped off their dragons and headed to the Training Room. The section where Griffith taught lessons was kind of like a cave.

Most days, everyone wanted to be outside in the Valley of Clouds. Drake loved it there because it reminded him of working in his family's onion fields. But today, nobody was complaining about staying inside. Everyone wanted to help Kepri.

When they walked into the classroom, they saw a giant pile of books on the table.

"Everyone take a book," Griffith said, pointing to a stack of books. "A dark

wizard made that orb. So we must find a cure for Sun Dragons who have been touched by dark magic. Quickly, now!" He was already flipping through *All About Sun Dragons*.

Drake took *Dragons 101* back to his desk. The room was quiet, except for the sound of turning pages. Drake read and read, but couldn't find anything. No one could.

Then Rori held up *Dragon Lore*. "I found something!" she cried. "Listen: 'Each Sun Dragon is born with a Moon Dragon twin. These twins can cure each other of almost anything.' Is this true? Does Kepri have a Moon Dragon twin?"

Griffith frowned. "I do not know. And if she does have a twin, that twin is likely very far away from here. There's no way we could find the Moon Dragon in time."

Ana stood up. "Well, my book has a potion in it called Wicked-Away," she said. "It heals creatures harmed by dark magic."

She brought the book to Griffith. His eyes lit up.

"This might do it! It's not just for Sun Dragons so I'm not sure if it will work. But it's worth a try," he said. "Drake and Bo, go to my workshop. Bring back a jar of moonbeams and a sack of sunflower seeds. Hurry!"

The boys raced into the hall to Griffith's workshop. The workshop was filled with bottles and jars. The bottles and jars were stuffed with strange plants and filled with potions.

Drake walked to the left side of the room, and Bo took the right side. Drake picked up a jar with purple liquid inside.

"Lily dew," he read out loud. He checked a few more jars—and then saw something glowing on the top shelf. Standing on his toes, he grabbed it.

A pale blue light shimmered inside the jar. Drake read the label.

"Moonbeams! I've got them!" he shouted.

"And I've got the seeds," Bo said. "Let's go!"

When they got back to the classroom, Rori was stirring liquid in a black metal pot. Ana was reading directions aloud from her book. Griffith clapped his hands when he saw the two boys.

"That was fast! Now, let's make this healing potion," said Griffith. "Drake, empty the jar into the pot. Bo, add three seeds, please."

Drake carefully opened the jar lid. The moonbeams slid out like water. Then Bo dropped in three black seeds.

"Keep stirring, Rori," Griffith said.

Rori stirred. The liquid turned blue and started to shine. A soft light came from the pot. Griffith scooped up some liquid with a ladle and put it in a clean jar.

"Will this potion make Kepri feel better?" Bo asked.

"There's only one way to find out," Griffith said.

They all walked to Kepri's cave. Her eyes were closed, and her yellow scales had lost their shine.

Griffith handed the jar to Ana. "You are her Dragon Master. She will listen to you. She must drink this," he said.

Ana nodded. She walked up to Kepri. "I have something for you," she said softly.

Kepri opened her eyes. She smiled when she saw Ana. "We made it for you—to make you well again," Ana said, holding up the jar.

Kepri opened her mouth. Ana slowly poured the potion inside.

"This has got to work," she whispered.

ANA'S STORY

The Dragon Masters crowded around Kepri.

"Feel better?" Ana asked her dragon. But Kepri just closed her eyes again.

Bo looked at Griffith. "Will the potion work right away?"

"I do not know," Griffith said. "We must wait and see. You all should head to dinner while I stay with Kepri."

"I'm not leaving her," Ana said firmly.

Griffith put a gentle hand on her shoulder. "Ana, you must take care of yourself," he said. "You must stay strong for Kepri. I will send for you if anything changes."

The Dragon Masters left the cave, leaving a worried wizard and a sick dragon behind them.

Up in the dining room, they all picked at their dinner. Ana only ate a few bites of food. Drake ate some carrots and chicken—but only about half as much as usual. Bo stared at his plate. Even Rori was quiet for a change.

Then the door at the end of the room banged open. One of the king's soldiers walked in.

"Do you have news about Kepri?" Ana asked.

The soldier walked over to Drake without saying a word. He handed him a rolled-up piece of paper.

Drake opened it. "It's a letter from my mom!"

Dear Drake,
    It is good here in the
fields. The onions are big.
    I know you are busy
helping the king with his
special project. But I miss
you. Work hard!
        Love
    Your Mother

Drake felt tears sting his eyes. He knew he
was doing important work for the king, but
he still missed his mom.

"I wish I could tell my family about the dragons," Drake said.

"They have to be kept a secret," Rori warned.

"I wish my father would write to me more often," Ana said. "I'd like to hear about his adventures."

"What kind of adventures?" Bo asked.

"My father sells beautiful fabrics," she said. "He travels all over far-away lands selling them. And we lived near the pyramids, so I often went there with him."

"What's a pyramid?" Rori asked.

"It holds a king's body after he dies. It's sort
of shaped like this." Ana made a triangle shape
with her hands. "The pyramids are bigger than
anything you've ever seen."

"Your dad's adventures sound amazing,"
said Drake.

"They are." Ana sighed. "But they're also dangerous. There are many robbers on the roads. The robbers steal from people who have goods to sell—like our fabrics. And they often steal gold and other treasures from the pyramids. That is why my father did not argue when King Roland's men came for me. He knew I would be safer elsewhere."

Ana looked sad. Bo was quiet.

I guess everyone else is just as homesick as I am, Drake thought.

After dinner, Drake and Bo went to the room that they shared. Drake climbed into bed and fell asleep right away. He dreamed of rivers and big tombs shaped like triangles. Then the desert sky turned green . . . bright green. Drake woke up.

The green Dragon Stone around his neck was glowing brightly.

Worm needs me! Drake thought.

Then he heard Worm's voice inside his mind. *Come now!*

WORM CALLS

Drake jumped out of bed. He shook Bo awake.

"Worm needs us!" Drake cried.

That was all Bo needed to hear. The boys raced downstairs to the door that led to the dragon training area. Drake tried to open it.

"It's locked!" Drake cried.

"Good thing I have a key," said a voice.

Drake and Bo turned around. Rori and Ana were standing there. Rori held up a key.

"Where did you get that?" Drake asked.

"I swiped it from one of the castle guards when I first got here," Rori said. "It's a skeleton key. It opens up *all* the locks in the castle."

"We came running as soon as we heard you two stomping down the hall!" Ana added. "We figured something was up."

"I'm glad you came. But please hurry!" Drake said.

Rori opened the door.

When they got to Kepri's cave, Worm was in front of it.

How did Worm get out of his cave? Drake wondered.

"Worm, what's wrong?" he asked.

Worm nodded toward Kepri. The gate to her cave was open and the Dragon Masters stepped inside. Griffith was asleep in the corner. Books were piled around him.

Kepri was asleep, too—but she looked sicker than before. Her scales looked dull. She looked thin and pale. Her breathing was loud and heavy.

The Dragon Masters were stunned.

"She wasn't this sick earlier," Rori said. "Did the potion make her worse?"

"Maybe it just didn't work," Bo said.

"We have to *do something!*" Ana cried.

Drake looked at Worm.

"Isn't there anything we can do?" Drake whispered.

Worm's body began to glow. Drake wasn't sure why, but he knew just what to do. He put one hand on Worm's snout and one hand on Kepri's tail.

"Everybody, touch Worm! Now!" he yelled.

Startled, his friends obeyed. They all laid their hands on Worm.

Griffith's eyes snapped open.

"What is going on?" the wizard asked.

But before Drake could answer, green light exploded in the room, blinding them.

FAR-AWAY LANDS

Drake felt weird. He couldn't feel the ground under his feet. But he could still feel his hand on Worm. His stomach did a flip-flop.

Then the green light faded. Drake blinked. His feet landed on sand, and he could feel cool air on his face.

Worm, Kepri, and the Dragon Masters were standing on a pathway. A white stone wall lined one side of the path. On the other side of them was a tall, strangely shaped building. Griffith was not with them.

Worm, why did you bring us here? Drake wondered.

Drake looked up at the big building. Each of the building's four sides was shaped like a triangle. The pointy top was capped with shining gold.

Ana's eyes got wide. "A pyramid!" she cried.

"Drake, what have you done? Where are we?" Rori asked. She sounded scared.

Ana turned to her. "I think we are in my homeland."

"But how . . . ?" Drake started to say. Then he looked at Worm. The dragon's green eyes were shining. "Worm must have used his mind powers to bring us here!"

"That's impossible!" said Rori. "Dragons can't travel halfway across the world using their minds."

"Look around you, Rori," Bo said. "It must be possible. We are no longer in the Kingdom of Bracken."

"But why didn't Worm bring Vulcan and Shu with us?" Rori asked.

Drake thought back to Kepri's cave. "We were all touching Worm. And I was touching Kepri. But the other dragons were still in their caves."

"And now we are here, in the land where Kepri and I were born," said Ana.

"Wait! Remember what I read in Griffith's book—about Sun Dragon twins?" Rori asked, her voice getting excited. "It said that every Sun Dragon has a Moon Dragon twin that can heal it."

"So Kepri's twin might be here!" said Bo.

"Do you think that's why Worm brought us here?" asked Drake.

Suddenly, they heard loud voices. The voices came from the other side of the stone wall. Drake didn't understand the language.

But Ana did. "Oh, no! Robbers! They often come to the pyramids to steal things. That must be why they are here! We cannot let anyone see us—or our dragons!"

"But there's nowhere to hide!" said Bo.

Just then, a boy stepped out from the shadows. He had golden-brown skin and black hair, like Ana.

"Follow me!" he said.

A STRANGE BOY

Rori stepped closer to the boy. "Why should we follow you?" she asked. "We don't even know you!"

"Trust me," the boy said, just as the robbers' voices grew louder. "I am surprised to see that you have dragons. But I know how to keep them safe. Come on!"

"We must hurry!" Ana said.

They had no choice. The boy waved for them to follow him. He touched the pyramid. One of the big stones pushed in, revealing an opening.

A secret door! Drake thought.

"Inside, quick!" the boy said. "Dragons first."

He stepped aside to let them in. Kepri was weak, but Worm nudged her gently with his nose. She stepped through the door. As Drake walked past the boy, he saw a cord around the boy's neck. Something green and sparkling was dangling from the cord.

A Dragon Stone!

The boy slipped in behind Drake and the secret door closed. They were inside a dark tunnel. Flaming torches lined the walls.

Drake turned to the boy.

"Who are you? Are you a Dragon Master, too?" He pointed to the green stone around the boy's neck. Ana, Rori, and Bo gasped when they saw it.

The boy smiled. "My name is Heru," he said. "I do not know what a Dragon Master is. My father gave me this stone."

"King Roland calls us Dragon Masters," Drake explained. "We were chosen by the Dragon Stone to work with dragons."

"I have not heard of King Roland. Are you from far away?" Heru asked.

Bo nodded. "Very far."

Heru frowned. "How strange. Can you tell me why Wati brought me here tonight?"

Ana was stroking Kepri's neck. The dragon's eyes seemed brighter now that she was inside the pyramid.

"Who's Wati?" Drake asked.

Heru grinned. "He is my dragon."

By now they had left the tunnel. They were inside a dark room. Drake looked up. The ceiling was so far above that he couldn't see it. Then something appeared out of the darkness. A huge, black dragon flew down from the ceiling. His eyes glowed bright yellow.

"*Aaaiieeeee!*"

With a loud cry, the dragon flew down, charging right at them!

KEPRI AND WATI

et down, everyone!" Drake yelled. The Dragon Masters all ducked. But the dragon was not after them.

He came to a stop right next to Kepri. The dragon wrapped his wings around her and made a happy, purring sound.

"It looks like they know each other," Drake said, pointing to the two dragons.

Wati was gently stroking Kepri's back with one of his wings. Her eyes were closed, and her head was drooping. Wati had black scales, and Kepri had white scales. But they had the same graceful bodies and yellow-tipped wings.

"They look a lot alike," said Bo.

"Yes, except that Kepri has light scales and Wati has dark scales," added Drake. "Light and dark—"

"Like the sun and the moon!" Rori yelled.

Ana's mouth dropped open. "This is what we'd been hoping for!"

Heru looked thrilled. "Wati is a Moon Dragon. My father taught me that all Moon Dragons have a twin—a Sun Dragon," he said. "Wati must have known that Kepri would be in this pyramid tonight. That explains why he suddenly flew off earlier. I am glad that I followed him here."

Drake was starting to figure it out. "So, Kepri must have known that Wati could heal her," he said. "And she must have told Worm about her twin. That's how Worm knew to bring her here!"

"Is Worm an Earth Dragon?" Heru asked.

Drake nodded.

"They have amazing powers," said Heru. "Worm did the right thing when he brought Kepri here."

Rori gave Drake a high five. Ana hugged Worm. "Thank you, Worm!"

Then Bo looked nervously at Kepri and Wati. "Look!"

Wati was standing up on his hind legs with his wings spread out wide.

"Everyone, step back, quick!" Heru yelled.

They moved away just as Wati opened his mouth. A ribbon of dark colors streamed out.

It looks almost like a rainbow, Drake thought, *except it's all blue and black and purple.*

Wati's rainbow ribbon grew and grew. It swirled around Kepri's body. She stirred a little, but her eyes were still closed.

Ana squeezed Drake's hand.

The light from the blue-and-purple rainbow grew bigger and shone brighter. The Dragon Masters had to shield their eyes.

Then . . . *whoosh!* The light swirled all around them.

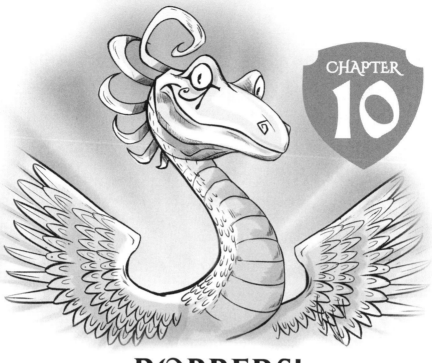

ROBBERS!

he light began to fade. Drake blinked. Everyone looked at Kepri. Her white scales looked shiny again. Her eyes were open and clear. She did not look sick anymore, just a little tired.

"Kepri!" Ana cried happily. She started to run to her when—

Bam! They heard the sound of wood breaking. Loud voices were coming from the tunnel that led to the hidden chamber.

"The robbers are coming!" Ana yelled. "We must get out of here!"

Rori balled her hands into fists. "We'll fight them!" she growled.

Kepri and Wati roared as four men dressed in black ran into the chamber. They carried bows and arrows, spears, and clubs.

When the robbers saw the dragons, they stopped, their eyes wide. Then one of the men started yelling to the others. The men raised their weapons and took aim at the dragons.

"They want to capture the dragons!" Ana warned.

Wati quickly sprang into action. He shot a black beam of light from his mouth. The beam hit the first robber in the chest and knocked him down.

Drake's heart pounded. He moved closer to Worm.

Then the second robber stepped forward. He sent an arrow flying right at Kepri.

"No!" Ana cried. Then she jumped in the path of the arrow!

FLYING

Drake watched in horror as the arrow flew toward Ana. He dove toward her, hoping to knock her out of the way. But before he could reach her, the arrow stopped in midair—inches from Ana's face.

Drake landed with a thud. He picked himself up and looked at Worm. The dragon's green eyes were glowing. Drake knew what that meant: Worm had used his mind powers to stop the arrow.

The arrow fell to the floor. And Worm wasn't finished! Next the weapons flew from the hands of the robbers. They slammed into the wall, breaking into pieces.

The four robbers
floated up off the floor.
Their legs dangled
beneath them. They
shouted at Worm.

Drake could see the
green light in Worm's
eyes starting to flicker.

"Worm can't hold them up there much
longer," he guessed. "We must get out of here!"

"Get on the dragons!" Heru yelled.

Heru and Rori climbed onto Wati. Ana
climbed onto Kepri's back. Drake and Bo
climbed onto Worm.

"Wati! Blast the top of the pyramid!" Heru
ordered.

Wati aimed a black beam of light at the top
of the chamber. A bright rainbow ribbon came
from Kepri's mouth and joined it. The top of
the pyramid opened up!

"Now we fly out," Heru said. "Go!"

Wati flew up, and Kepri flew up behind him. Worm stayed on the ground. The light in his eyes kept flickering. The robbers' feet were almost touching the floor now.

Drake saw that Worm couldn't use his power to do too many things at once. He knew his dragon couldn't fly like the other dragons. But Worm could take them somewhere else in a flash—if he was strong enough.

"Worm, get us out of here!" Drake yelled.

Worm let go of his grip on the robbers. They tumbled to the floor. Then they quickly got up, angrily charging toward Drake, Bo, and Worm. The dragon's eyes glowed green.

"Hold on tight, Bo!" Drake yelled.

One second, they were in the chamber. The next, they were outside the pyramid!

ANA'S DECISION

Drake and Bo climbed off Worm's back. They looked up. The sun was just starting to rise. Kepri and Wati were flying around.

"We can't stay here long," Bo said. "Soon the villagers will wake up, and we can't let them see the dragons."

Drake nodded. "Yes, and Griffith is probably worried about us."

Kepri and Wati glided down and landed next to them. Ana, Heru, and Rori climbed off the dragons' backs. They ran over to Drake and Bo.

"You made it!" Ana cried.

"We figured that Worm could do his cool Earth-Dragon-thing and get you out of there in a blink," Rori said.

Drake smiled at Worm. "Yeah, he's awesome."

Then the twin dragons flew up again and circled the golden top of the pyramid.

"Kepri and Wati look so happy together," Bo said.

Ana sighed. "I am so glad Kepri is better," she said. "It's all because of Wati. He knew how to heal her when no one else could. I really think she should stay here with him." She sounded sad.

"But she's *your* dragon," Drake said. "She should stay with *you.*"

Ana shook her head. "I don't have a strong connection with Kepri. Not like the one that you have with Worm. Your stone glows when you and Worm connect—just like earlier tonight when he called to you. My Dragon Stone has never glowed."

"But Griffith said it would happen to you, too," Drake said. He looked at Bo and Rori. "To all of you."

Ana had tears in her eyes. "I might never know now. It seems like Kepri is better off without me."

Heru put a hand on her shoulder. "Listen to Drake, Ana. I knew Wati for a year before my stone glowed," he said. "It takes patience."

Drake turned to Heru. "You said you weren't a Dragon Master. But you have a Dragon Stone and your own dragon. How are you *not* a Dragon Master?"

Heru shrugged. "It is *your* king who has called you a Dragon Master. I serve no king. All I know is that for many ages, my family has served dragons. When dragons come to us, we help them."

King Roland doesn't want to help dragons,
Drake thought. *He just wants us to train them.*

"We must get back to our kingdom," Bo said.
"The castle will be waking up soon. If King
Roland finds the dragons missing . . ."

Drake shuddered. "That would be bad for
us—and for Griffith!"

He turned to Ana. "We must go. Do you
want to see if Kepri will come with us?"

"I've decided that she should stay with
Wati," Ana said sadly. "I will say good-bye. Let
me call her."

ONE LAST GOOD-BYE

Wait!" Drake yelled. He saw something: the Dragon Stone on Ana's neck. It was glowing! Drake pointed to it. Bo, Rori, and Heru all turned to look.

"Ana, your stone!" they cried.

Ana gazed down at the glowing stone. She got a strange look in her eyes.

"Ana, what is it?" Rori asked.

"I think I can hear Kepri's voice…inside my head!" Ana said.

Everyone was quiet as Ana listened. She got a smile on her face. She looked up at Kepri flying in the sky.

"Kepri wants to come back to be with her brother  one day," Ana said. "Just like I want to come back to my family. But until then, she wants to stay with me in the kingdom of Bracken."

"I'm so happy for you," said Drake.

"Yes. We would all miss Kepri as much as you," added Rori.

The sun was higher in the sky now.

"Ana, we must go," said Bo softly. "Everyone, including our king, will be waking up soon."

Ana nodded. "Come, Kepri," she called out.

Kepri and Wati circled the pyramid one last time. Then both dragons swooped down. They landed next to Worm and the Dragon Masters.

Drake smiled at Heru. "Thank you for helping us," he said.

Heru smiled. "No problem. Perhaps we will meet again."

"That would be nice," Drake said. He turned to his friends. "Okay, everyone. Just like last time. Place one hand on Worm."

Ana hugged Wati. Her cheeks were shiny with tears as she broke away. Then she put one hand on Kepri and one hand on Worm.

"Okay, Worm," Drake said. "Home, please."

Worm's body started to glow green once more . . .

HOME

few seconds later, the Dragon Masters were all back in the Training Room in King Roland's castle.

"Good heavens!" a voice cried.

When Worm's light faded, Drake saw Griffith standing in front of them—with another wizard! Like Griffith, he had a white beard. But he was a head shorter than Griffith and twice as round.

Griffith looked at Kepri. "My goodness! She is cured!" he said. "When I saw Worm glow green and you all vanished, I trusted that Worm would know where to find a cure."

"Yes! Worm took us to meet Kepri's twin, a Moon Dragon named Wati," Drake explained. "Wati cured her."

"Just like it said in *Dragon Lore*!" Rori added.

Griffith put his hands together. "Wonderful!" he cried. "Worm, you are full of surprises."

"He is very unusual," said the shorter wizard, stepping up close to Worm.

"Dragon Masters, meet Diego," Griffith said, pointing to the wizard.

"Very nice to meet you," Diego said.

"I have asked Diego for his help," Griffith said. "We have been trying to find out which dark wizard could have sent that red orb."

"I know only one wizard with a heart evil enough for this type of dark magic," Diego said. "His name is Maldred."

Drake shivered. "Why would Maldred send the orb here?"

"That's something we still have to figure out," Griffith said.

Diego put an arm on Griffith's shoulder. "Together."

Everyone was quiet as they thought about this. Then the loud voice of a castle guard broke the silence.

"All rise for King Roland!"

Diego snapped his fingers and vanished in a puff of smoke. Then the king stomped in with two guards behind him.

"Did you heal my dragon, wizard?" King Roland asked.

Drake thought quickly. If the king found out that Worm had taken them far away, he might get mad. Or he might try to use Worm's special power. *What if he takes Worm away from me?*

"Griffith made a potion, and it worked," Drake lied. He pointed to Kepri. "See?"

"I didn't ask you, boy," King Roland said crossly.

But the king's frown faded when he saw Kepri. "Hmm. I see it's true. Good work, wizard. It looks like I won't have to replace you with another wizard . . . for now."

Then the king and his guards turned and left.

Griffith smiled at Drake. "Thank you," he said.

"Will you tell the king about that dark wizard named Maldred?" Bo asked.

"There is not much his army can do against Maldred's dark magic," Griffith said. "It will be up to us to protect this kingdom."

Rori snorted. "Vulcan won't be afraid of some old wizard."

"And Vulcan won't be fighting that wizard alone," Ana said, looking at Kepri. "All of us will help."

Drake looked at Worm. He was proud of how his dragon had helped Kepri. "Yes," he said, turning to his friends. "Whatever happens, we're all in this together!"

DRAGON MASTERS
SAVING THE SUN DRAGON

Questions and Activities

Name some similarities between the Dragon Masters and their dragons. For example, how is Bo similar to Shu?

What **CAUSES** Kepri to get sick?

Who are Heru and Wati? Why are they important?

Why does Drake **LIE** to King Roland on page 184?

Do you think Kepri belongs with Ana or with Wati? Why? Write about your opinion.

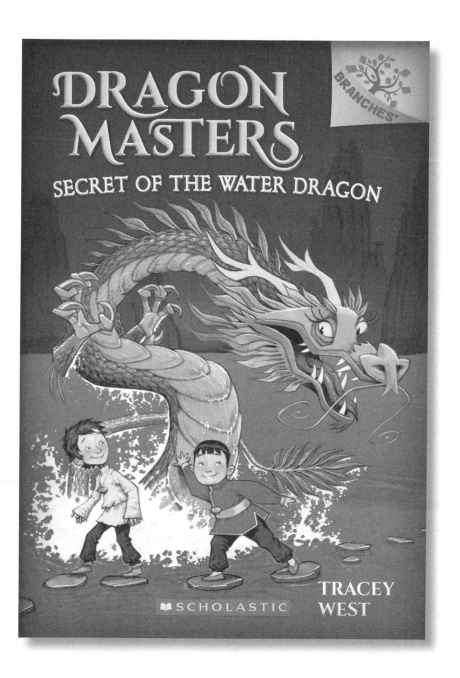

TABLE OF CONTENTS

1. SADDLE UP! 191
2. THE BLACK FEATHER 197
3. A THIEF IN THE CASTLE! 202
4. THE WIZARD'S TRAP 208
5. BO'S STORY 214
6. THE RAVEN GUARD 219
7. THE CHASE 225
8. SHU TO THE RESCUE 236
9. GRIFFITH'S PLAN 240
10. ACROSS THE WORLD 245
11. EMPEROR SONG 252
12. THE WATER DRAGON'S POWER .. 259
13. BATTLE OF THE ORBS 267
14. RISE AGAINST MALDRED 273

CHAPTER 1

SADDLE UP!

teady now," warned Griffith, the king's wizard. "We have never tried putting a saddle on a dragon before. I am not sure how she will like it."

Griffith and the Dragon Masters were in the Training Room, hidden beneath King Roland's castle. A magical stone called the Dragon Stone had chosen Drake, Bo, Rori, and Ana to work with dragons. Griffith was their teacher. The Dragon Masters stood around a big dragon with shiny blue scales.

"Bo, bring the buckle under Shu's belly," Griffith said. "Now tighten the buckle. Good!"

Drake watched his friend Bo put the saddle on Shu. She was a Water Dragon, so she was usually very calm. Shu stood still as Bo pulled the buckle tightly.

"Good job, Shu," Bo said, patting her neck.

"Now can I put a saddle on Vulcan?" asked Rori.

"And can we please ride our dragons today, Griffith?" asked Ana.

"King Roland's crafters are making a saddle for each dragon," answered Griffith. "The other saddles will be ready tomorrow."

"Will there be a saddle for Worm?" asked Drake. He looked over at his dragon. Worm was an Earth Dragon. He had a long body, like a snake. He had no legs, and tiny wings. Worm couldn't fly like the other dragons could.

"Yes. Worm has a very special power. He can take you from one place to another in the blink of an eye," Griffith said. "A saddle is a good idea for any type of travel."

Drake nodded.

"It is time for dinner," said Griffith. "Please put away your dragons and head to the dining room."

"Well, I hope *I* get to test Vulcan's saddle *first* tomorrow," Rori said. "Vulcan and I didn't get to do anything fun today."

She marched off toward the Dragon Caves. Her dragon, Vulcan, stomped after her. He was a Fire Dragon with red scales.

Ana followed Rori. She skipped along. Her dragon, Kepri, moved like a graceful dancer beside her. Kepri was a Sun Dragon with a slim body and white scales.

Drake helped Bo take off Shu's saddle. They put their dragons in their caves. Then they took the stairs to the dining room in the tower. After dinner, the boys went to their room.

Drake touched his Dragon Stone as they walked. Each of the Dragon Masters wore a piece of the stone. It let them connect with their dragons.

"Bo," Drake said, "do you think Worm can go anywhere in the world?"

"I think so," Bo said. "He has very strong powers."

Bo opened the door. Then he froze. Drake bumped into him.

"Bo, what's wrong?" Drake asked. His friend was staring at his bed. His face looked pale.

Drake followed his gaze. A black feather lay on Bo's pillow.

THE BLACK FEATHER

hat's strange," Drake said. "We must've left the window open."

Bo sat down on the bed and picked up the feather. He looked worried.

"Bo, it's just a feather," Drake said. "What's wrong?"

"Nothing. I am fine," Bo said.

But Drake didn't believe him.

Bo was quiet as the boys climbed into bed. He rolled over and faced the wall.

Drake could tell that something was bothering Bo. *But why would a feather upset him?*

Drake drifted off to sleep, thinking about his friend: *I hope he's okay.*

When Drake woke up in the morning, Bo was sitting up in bed. He was wide-awake.

"Wow! Have you been up a long time?" said Drake.

Bo shrugged. "Um . . . I'm just excited to ride Shu today."

But Drake did not hear excitement in Bo's voice.

The boys headed down to breakfast. Ana and Rori were already eating.

"It's about time you two sleepyheads got here," said Rori.

"I can't wait to get outside!" said Ana. "Last night, Kepri sent a picture to my mind. We were flying in the sky. She sends me lots of pictures since we made our connection."

Drake nodded. He and Worm had formed a strong connection, too. He could hear Worm in his head. His Dragon Stone glowed green every time it happened. But this hadn't happened for Bo and Shu yet. Or for Rori and Vulcan.

"I'm sure we will go right outside. Where is Griffith?" Bo asked, looking around.

Rori shrugged. "He's probably getting the saddles ready. Hurry up and eat!"

Drake was excited to test out Worm's saddle. He wolfed down his breakfast.

"Let's go!" Rori said as soon as Drake was done. Drake got up and put an apple in his pocket to give Worm. Ana grabbed Bo's arm and pulled him off his seat. As they left, Drake looked back. Bo had hardly eaten breakfast.

Downstairs, they found Griffith waiting for them in the Training Room. He had a serious look on his face.

"What's wrong?" Ana asked.

"Somebody tried to steal the Dragon Stone!" he said.

A THIEF IN THE CASTLE!

The Dragon Masters gasped.

"What happened?" Rori asked.

"I always protect the stone with magic charms," Griffith explained. "These charms cannot be seen. But they form an invisible net around the box that holds the Dragon Stone. And they can only be broken with a magic spell."

"So how do you know someone tried to steal the stone?" asked Drake.

"This morning, I found that something had upset the magic of the charms. They were not broken, but I could tell that someone had tried to break them," Griffith answered.

Ana gripped the stone around her neck. "If somebody steals the main Dragon Stone would our smaller stones lose their powers?"

"No," the wizard replied. "But someone could use the main stone to control the dragons. Or even to form a dragon army."

"Isn't that what King Roland is doing?" asked Drake.

"King Roland wants to use the dragons for good. I have known King Roland since he was a boy. He is a good man at heart. And as long as the stone is in my care, I can keep it safe. Safe from people like Maldred..." He shuddered.

The Dragon Masters looked at one another.

"You mean Maldred the dark wizard? Is he the one who tried to steal the Dragon Stone last night?" Drake asked.

The Dragon Masters all knew that Maldred had tried to get to their dragons before. They had never seen Maldred. But already, his dark magic had caused a lot of trouble.

Griffith shook his head. "No," he said. "Maldred would not have been so careless. He would have broken the charms using a spell. Our thief clearly did not know about the charms."

Drake glanced at Bo. His friend kept looking nervously over his shoulder.

"To protect the Dragon Stone, I must find a better hiding place for it," Griffith continued. "I will leave the castle right away to look for one."

"So there's no riding practice today?" Ana asked. She looked at the finished saddles.

"You may go outside and have a free day. But the dragons must stay inside," he said. Then he hurried out of the room.

"What do we do now?" Rori asked.

"Well, we can still spend the day with our dragons," Drake replied. "We can hang out with them in the caves."

"I — I must go," Bo said. "There is something I must take care of."

"What —" Drake began. But Bo was already rushing off.

"*He's* acting strange," Rori said, with her hands on her hips.

Ana nodded. "Yes, he seems quieter than usual today."

"I think something is worrying him," Drake said, remembering the black feather.

"Maybe he's worried about the Dragon Stone," said Rori.

As they headed to the Dragon Caves, Drake kept looking behind him.

Was the thief still in the castle?

THE WIZARD'S TRAP

Worm looked up as soon as Drake reached his cave. Drake took the apple from breakfast out of his pocket.

"Good morning, Worm," Drake said, holding out the treat. The dragon craned his long neck. He grabbed the apple in his teeth and ate it in one gulp.

208

Drake sat down on the cold floor of the cave.

"Somebody tried to steal the Dragon Stone last night," Drake said. "Griffith is finding a new hiding place for the stone. So we have a free day."

Rori and Ana walked up to Worm's cave.

"Come on, Drake! We're going outside," Rori said.

"Yeah, we don't want to be stuck in here all day," said Ana. "Coming?"

Drake shook his head. "No, thanks. I'm going to stay with Worm."

Rori shrugged. "Have fun in the dark! We'll be outside!"

The girls walked away. Drake started to tell Worm a story about when he lived back on the onion farm. Suddenly, Worm's neck jerked up. His eyes glowed green.

"What is it, Worm?" asked Drake.

Drake's Dragon Stone glowed, too. Then he heard Worm's voice in his head.

Bo.

"What about Bo? Is he in trouble?" Drake asked.

Worm nodded.

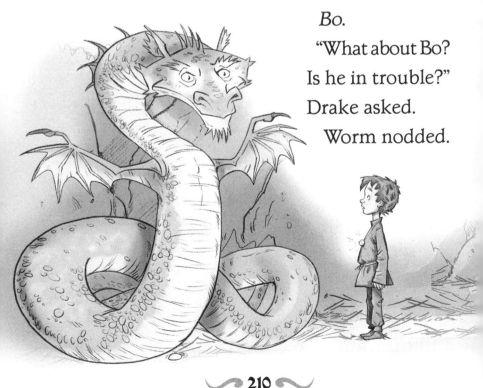

Drake jumped up. He ran out of the caves and through the Training Room. He was on the way to their room when he heard noises coming from inside Griffith's workshop. But he knew Griffith had left the castle.

Is someone in there? Drake wondered.

The door was open a crack. He peeked inside.

Bo was in Griffith's workshop — with one hand on the box that held the Dragon Stone!

Drake held back a gasp. Bo was reading aloud from a book. The words sounded magical, like something a wizard would say. *The charms protecting the stone could only be broken by a magic spell*, he remembered. Then a terrible thought hit him: *Is Bo trying to steal the Dragon Stone?!*

Drake pushed open the door. He had to stop Bo!

Suddenly, sparks shot out from the corner of the room. They hit the book Bo was holding and it fell to the ground. Griffith stepped out of the shadows. His finger was pointed at Bo.

"Stop, thief!"

BO'S STORY

Bo's hands were shaking. He looked up at Griffith.

Drake stood frozen in the doorway.

"Come in, Drake," Griffith said. Drake obeyed. The wizard's eyes stayed on Bo. "This is very serious. I set this trap because I thought someone *inside* the castle had tried to steal the stone last night. I said I was leaving the castle, but then I hid in here. I had to see if the thief would come back. And he did — *you* did."

Bo looked down at his shoes. "I am sorry," he said softly.

"Bo, tell me why you would do such a thing," Griffith said.

"I . . ." Bo looked up. "I cannot say."

"Please, Bo!" Drake blurted out. "I *know* you! You wouldn't steal anything. You have to explain."

Griffith looked into Bo's eyes. "We can help you, Bo," he said. "But you must tell us why you tried to steal the stone."

Bo sighed. "It began when King Roland's soldiers came to my kingdom. They went to see Emperor Song."

"What did they want?" Drake asked.

"They wanted *me*," Bo replied. "The soldiers told the emperor that King Roland wanted me for an important project. At first, Emperor Song did not agree to send me off. He was worried that I would not be safe. But my parents said it would be an honor to our kingdom. So he agreed."

Drake nodded. "Emperor Song sounds very kind."

"He is — or at least, he used to be," Bo said. "Last night, I found a black feather on my pillow. There was a note with it that I did not show Drake."

He took a piece of paper from his pocket and gave it to Griffith.

"It says —" His voice choked. "It says that Emperor Song has put my family in prison. To save them, I must steal the Dragon Stone and bring it to him right away. And I must not tell anyone." His eyes filled with tears.

Griffith put a hand on his shoulder. "I understand."

"But you said he was a kind emperor, Bo," Drake said. "Why would he do this?"

"I do not know," Bo replied. "I fear that some evil has come over him."

"I fear you are right," said the wizard. "And we must help your emperor. But first, we have a problem closer to home. The black feather is a symbol of the Raven Guard."

Bo nodded. "Yes. You have heard of them?"

"I have heard stories," Griffith said. "The Raven Guard is a group of skilled fighters who serve the emperor. They are very dangerous."

Drake turned pale. "So if the feather is in the castle . . ."

"Then one of the Raven Guards is here, too!" said Bo.

THE RAVEN GUARD

What do you know about the Raven Guards, Bo?" asked Griffith.

"They dress all in black," said Bo. "They can move silently without being seen."

"They *must* be sneaky," said Drake. "How else could one of them get that feather on your pillow?"

Bo nodded. "They are very skilled at spying."

Just then, Drake's Dragon Stone felt warm on his skin. He looked down. It was glowing! Then he heard Worm's voice inside his head.

Danger outside!

"Rori and Ana!" Drake cried. "They went outside by themselves!"

Griffith frowned. "We must find them." He stomped into the hallway and yelled to the guard by the Training Room door. "Simon, please watch my workshop! Make sure no one enters!"

Simon grunted in reply, and the three of them rushed out of the workshop. They raced through the long tunnel that led to the Valley of Clouds.

When they got outside, Rori and Ana ran up to them. They both started talking quickly.

"The thief was here! He was dressed in black!" cried Ana.

"He had a red crystal! And he shone it in our eyes," Rori said.

"Then he started asking us stuff! And we gave him answers!" Ana said. "Somehow he *made* us tell the truth, even though we did not want to. I think the crystal was —"

"Magic!" Rori added. "And then he was gone! He moved so fast!"

"He is a skilled and dangerous spy," said Griffith. "The red crystal he used sounds like dark magic. Now, tell me: What questions did he ask?"

"He wanted to know where the Dragon Stone was," Ana replied. "And if it was guarded by anything."

"*Ana* told him about the magic charms!" Rori said.

"And *you* told him Griffith had left the castle," Ana said.

"Wait a minute, Griffith. What are you doing here?" Rori asked.

"Never mind that," Griffith said. "I am here now. And the spy may be on his way to steal the Dragon Stone. We must get to my workshop. Hurry!"

They all raced back through the tunnel. Drake's heart pounded.

When they got to Griffith's office, Simon the guard was conked out on the floor! And the workshop door was wide open!

THE CHASE

Griffith ran to the box that held the Dragon Stone. He opened the lid.

"The Dragon Stone is gone!" he cried.

"The Raven Guard must have come right for it," Bo said.

"Raven Guard? What do you mean, Bo?" Rori asked, her green eyes flashing. "What is going on?"

Bo told Rori and Ana everything — about the feather, the Raven Guard, and Emperor Song.

"So *you* tried to steal the stone last night?" Ana asked Bo. "And that spy came from *your* kingdom?"

Bo nodded.

"Now, Dragon Masters, we must act quickly," Griffith said. He picked up a small box and opened it. A green feather floated in the air.

"I put a magic Finding Charm on the Dragon Stone," he said. "This feather will lead us to it. But we must hurry!"

Bo nodded. "The Raven Guard moves swiftly."

"We will use our two fastest dragons — and their new saddles," Griffith said. "Rori, you and I will take Vulcan. Ana, you and Drake take Kepri."

"What about me?" asked Bo.

"You will stay here," said Griffith. "Make sure Simon is all right."

Bo nodded. "Yes, Griffith."

Drake and the others raced to the dragon caves. He and Ana quickly saddled Kepri and climbed on her back. Rori and Griffith climbed on Vulcan.

"Feather, find the stone!" Griffith commanded. The feather zipped toward the tunnels.

Vulcan took off after the feather like a shot. Kepri was on his tail. When the feather left the tunnels, the dragons took to the air. They flew across the Valley of Clouds.

Drake looked down. His stomach flipped.
"We're so high up!" he yelled to Ana.
"Isn't it amazing?!" she yelled back.

Wind brushed Drake's cheeks as the dragons
flew across the Valley of Clouds. They flew
over the hills, to the deep, wide forest beyond.

Drake kept his eyes on the feather. Up ahead, he could see something moving across the treetops: the Raven Guard! The small, black figure moved like the wind from one tree to the next.

Griffith saw him, too. So he plucked the Finding Feather from the air. He pointed down. Vulcan dove through the trees.

Drake's stomach flipped as Kepri followed. The two dragons glided side by side over the treetops.

"We're catching up to him!" Ana shouted, her dark eyes gleaming.

Vulcan was closest to the guard. The dragon opened his mouth wide.

"No, Vulcan!" Griffith yelled. "No fire! It's too dangerous! Ana, pull ahead with Kepri! Block the guard, and I will use a spell on him!"

"Faster, Kepri!" Ana told her dragon. "Get in front of that guy!"

Kepri picked up speed. She flew past the quickly moving guard. Then she turned around, blocking his path.

Drake saw that the guard wore all black. Only his eyes were showing. The guard reached into a pocket. He pulled out a handful of glittering, red dust.

Red: the color of dark magic. The color of the crystal that the guard had used to make Rori and Ana answer him.

The same color as the ball of light that Maldred had sent into the castle weeks ago.

The dust must be dark magic, too, Drake guessed.

"Ana! Turn Kepri back NOW!" he yelled. "It's dark magic!"

Dark magic makes Sun Dragons sick. Drake knew they had to get Kepri away from here before the red dust came near her.

Ana quickly steered Kepri away from the guard. Drake looked back at Griffith. The wizard's finger was pointed at the guard. He was starting to say a spell.

That's when Drake noticed the bag in the guard's hand.

The Dragon Stone must be in that bag! he thought.

"Rori! Grab the bag!" Drake yelled.

The guard quickly sprinkled red powder on himself.

Then everything happened at once.

Vulcan charged at the guard from behind. Rori reached out and yanked the bag out of the guard's hand. His eyes widened.

The red dust sparkled. Vulcan roared loudly. He blasted a stream of fire as the guard disappeared.

"Vulcan, no!" Rori cried.

The treetops burst into flame!

SHU TO THE RESCUE

Higher! Fly above the smoke!" Griffith yelled over the roar of the flames.

Vulcan and Kepri flew above the fire. Then a blue streak darted out in front of them.

It was Bo, riding his dragon! *But Bo isn't supposed to be outside!* thought Drake.

A powerful wave of water streamed out of Shu's mouth. The fire sizzled, then went out.

"I am sorry I did not stay behind," Bo told Griffith. "But when I looked outside and saw the smoke, Shu and I just had to help."

"You did well," Griffith told him. Bo smiled proudly.

"Rori, do you have the stone?" Griffith called out.

Rori opened the bag. The big, green Dragon Stone glittered inside.

"Got it!" she yelled back.

"Then to the castle! Hurry!" the wizard ordered.

They quickly flew back to the caves and climbed off the dragons.

"Bo, that was awesome!" said Ana. "Shu did a great job putting out that fire. And, Rori, you did a great job getting back the Dragon Stone."

"Thanks," Rori said. "Drake is the one who spotted it."

"So, how did that Raven guy just vanish?" Ana asked.

"He used the red dust to get away," Griffith said. "But he will not get far. He is using borrowed magic. It is not very strong."

"I am glad the Dragon Stone is safe," said Bo. "And I know we can't give it to Emperor Song. But I do not know what to do. He will keep my family in prison if we do not give the stone to him." He looked like he was about to cry.

Then Drake saw something. Bo's Dragon Stone was glowing!

"Bo, look!" he said, pointing.

Bo looked down. His eyes grew wide. He was quiet for a moment. Then a huge grin spread across his face.

"It's happening!" he cried. "Shu is speaking to me — inside my head!"

GRIFFITH'S PLAN

Bo closed his eyes, listening to his dragon.

"What is Shu saying?" Rori whispered.

"That there is a dark cloud over the emperor," Bo said, opening his eyes. "A darkness that is not his own."

240

"Could it be Maldred?" Drake asked, thinking of the dark wizard.

Griffith nodded. "The dust the guard used looks like Maldred's dark magic. Maldred may be using the emperor to get to the dragons."

"Can Shu help?" Ana asked.

"She says that she can," Bo replied, "but that she needs to see the emperor in person." He looked at Griffith. "May I bring her to him?"

"I do not know all the secrets a Water Dragon holds," Griffith said. "If Shu says she can help, then I trust her."

"We should go to your kingdom right now, Bo!" Drake said. "I'll get Worm."

"Let us think this through, Drake," Griffith said. "I trust you and Bo to go on your own. I must stay here to protect the Dragon Stone. Ana and Rori can assist me. But we will need the help of my friend, Diego, too."

Griffith snapped his fingers. *POOF!* Drake jumped. A cloud of smoke filled the room. When it cleared, a short, fat wizard was standing there.

"Griffith! What's wrong?" Diego asked.

"Maldred is trying to steal the Dragon Stone," Griffith explained. "You and I must strengthen the charms that protect it."

Diego nodded. "I will do whatever you need, my friend."

Griffith turned to Bo and Drake. "Be careful. Let Shu try to remove the dark cloud from Emperor Song. Make sure Bo's family is safe. Then come right back."

"We will do our best," Bo said.

Drake had a scary thought. *I know Bo feels bad about trying to steal the Dragon Stone. But what if the emperor tells Bo to do something else? Like turn over our dragons? Would he do it to save his family?*

Drake wasn't sure what to think. But right now, he had to trust his friend.

"There is no time to waste!" said Griffith. "Drake, put a saddle on Worm."

"I'll be fast!" Drake promised, and he ran to Worm's cave.

ACROSS THE WORLD

Worm, I need your help," Drake said. "We must go to the kingdom of Emperor Song. It might be dangerous, but we have to help the emperor and save Bo's family. Will you take us?"

Worm nodded. Drake quickly put his saddle on him. Then Bo rushed into the cave, riding Shu.

"Now, Drake, we just touch Worm for his power to work. Right?" Bo asked.

Drake nodded.

Bo touched Worm, and Shu touched Worm with her tail.

"Ready!" Bo said.

Drake took a deep breath. "Okay, Worm. Please take us to the kingdom of Emperor Song."

Worm's body started to glow. Green light filled the room. It grew brighter and brighter. Drake's heart raced.

The green light exploded. Drake felt weird. His stomach flip-flopped.

Then the light faded. He blinked. A moon shone in the sky above.

"We are here," said Bo.

"You did it, Worm!" Drake cheered.

He looked around. It was nighttime in the kingdom. A towering building rose up in front of them. Moonlight shone on a big, round pond in front of the building. Cherry trees lined the walkway around the pond.

Drake and Bo climbed down from their dragons.

"That is Emperor Song's palace," Bo said.

"We must bring Shu to him right away," Drake said.

"Yes. But he will be angry when he sees that I do not have the Dragon Stone," Bo said.

Drake shook his head. "I still don't get it, Bo," he said. "Why didn't you tell me what the feather meant? And about the note?"

"The note said not to tell anybody," Bo replied.

The boys walked away from the dragons as they talked.

"But I'm not anybody. I'm your *friend*," Drake shot back.

"Drake, I am sorry. I —" Bo stopped. A rustling sound came from the trees. "What was that?"

Drake looked up. He saw something move in the treetops. He held his breath.

"The Raven Guards!" Bo whispered.

Four guards dressed in black swooped down.

"Worm! Shu! Help us!" Drake yelled.

A dozen more guards dropped down around Worm and Shu.

Before the dragons could act, the Raven Guards carried Drake and Bo away with magical speed.

EMPEROR SONG

rake struggled as a Raven Guard held him under one arm.

"It is no use," Bo whispered. "They are much stronger than we are. We cannot fight them. And they are taking us to Emperor Song, which is what we want."

"But we need Shu!" Drake whispered back. "Do you think our dragons escaped those other guards?"

Bo frowned. "They may have been captured. We will have to face the emperor without them."

Drake looked down at his Dragon Stone.

Worm, give me a message.

But the stone didn't glow. Then Drake thought of something. *Emperor Song might see our pieces of the stone! What if he tries to take them?*

"Quick!" he whispered to Bo. "Hide your Dragon Stone."

The Raven Guards carried Drake and Bo through a large hall. Gleaming black and red stones formed a pattern on the floor. Large black columns lined the walls. A red dragon design swirled down the columns.

The guards took them to a large room. A dozen more Raven Guards waited for them there.

A man in a red robe sat on a white throne. He had a long mustache, a pointy black beard, and wore a black hat. A thin smile spread across his face when he saw Bo. It reminded Drake of a field snake's smile.

Bo whispered to Drake. "See the evil in his eyes? This is not the emperor I remember."

The guards let go of the boys and pushed them toward the emperor.

"Bo," Emperor Song said, "I am surprised that you came so quickly. Where is my Dragon Stone?"

Bo looked at Drake, panicked. They had been counting on Shu to help them deal with the emperor. Without Shu, they had no plan. And without Worm, there was no way out.

"Well, Bo?" the emperor asked. "I am waiting."

"I...I don't have the Dragon Stone, Emperor," Bo said in a small voice.

A dark look came over the emperor's face. "No Dragon Stone?! Then you have failed me!"

"It's not Bo's fault!" Drake blurted out.

Emperor Song looked down at Drake. "A child dares to speak to the emperor this way?! Take them to the prison! These boys shall join Bo's family."

Drake squeezed his eyes shut. *Worm? Worm? Can you hear me, Worm? We need help!*

"Take them away!" Emperor Song yelled. Then the doors burst open.

Swoooooooooooosh! A giant wave of water flooded the room!

THE WATER DRAGON'S POWER

The emperor jumped onto the seat of his throne. The strong wave knocked the guards off their feet. Drake held his breath, waiting to be knocked down, too. Then his whole body began to tingle. He looked down.

He was floating above the water! *But how?*

"It's the dragons!" Bo called out. Drake turned and saw that Bo was floating in midair, too. "Shu must have used the water from the pond to break into the castle. And Worm is keeping us above the water!"

Shu floated into the room, traveling on top of the waves. Her blue scales shimmered. Her eyes gleamed. Worm came behind her. As he slid across the floor, the water moved away from him.

Shu floated over to Bo. He climbed on her and gripped her saddle. Worm slid underneath Drake. Drake felt Worm's hold leave him, and he dropped right onto his dragon's saddle.

Emperor Song pointed at the two dragons. "Guards! Grab them!" he cried. But his Raven Guards were woozy after being hit by the wave. They slowly got to their feet, splashing in the knee-high water.

"More guards will come!" the emperor said. "You cannot harm me. I am the emperor! I am the ruler of this kingdom! Get back!"

Then Shu glided right up to the emperor. Her huge head stopped just inches away from his.

"Do not eat me!" Emperor Song yelled.

Shu closed her eyes. A misty blue cloud floated from her mouth. Emperor Song looked up at it, terrified. He froze as a light blue mist rained down on his head.

The look on his face changed. He looked peaceful.

"What a beautiful creature," the emperor said, reaching out. He gently touched Shu's nose.

Back on their feet, the Raven Guards charged toward Shu.

"STOP!" Emperor Song called out. "Our guests must not be harmed!"

Drake and Bo looked at each other.

"*Guests?*" Drake mouthed to Bo. It seemed like Shu's powers were working!

Emperor Song stood up. "I am sorry, Bo," he said. "I do not know what came over me. I should never have asked you to steal the Dragon Stone. I fear I was under a dark spell. But your dragon … your dragon has somehow saved me."

Bo's Dragon Stone began to glow beneath his shirt. Bo closed his eyes. After a minute, he opened them. "Shu has a very special, secret power. She can wash away any spell. She has just broken the spell that Maldred placed on you."

"I should never have let that wizard into the palace," said the emperor. "Maldred's dark spell made me force you to steal the Dragon Stone. My Raven Guards were only obeying my orders."

"Does this mean Bo's family will be safe?" Drake asked.

"Of course," Emperor Song said. "I will release them from prison."

Bo bowed his head. "Thank you, Emperor."

Drake smiled. He was happy for Bo.

Then, without warning, he heard Worm's voice in his head.

Danger is coming!

Drake looked up. A swarm of glowing red balls flew into the throne room. They came at them at lightning speed!

"It's Maldred's dark magic! Get down!" Drake yelled.

BATTLE
OF THE ORBS

The red balls of light darted around the room like angry bees.

Zap! One of the orbs shot a beam of dark energy at a Raven Guard. It knocked down the guard.

One of the orbs zoomed right at Drake. Worm's eyes glowed.

Boom! The orb exploded.

Another red ball zoomed toward Bo. *Bam!* The orb burst. Worm had used the power of his mind to destroy them.

Blast! Shu tried hitting one of the glowing balls with a jet of water. But the water bounced off it.

Around them, the Raven Guards were jumping and dodging. One swung a fighting stick at an orb. But like Shu's water, it didn't harm it at all.

Suddenly, the orbs grouped together. They zoomed all at once toward the dragons. Drake gripped Worm's saddle.

Boom! Boom! Boom! Worm blasted them with his green light, and they exploded.

Then the room became quiet. Drake looked around. Worm had destroyed all of the orbs!

"Good job, Worm," he said, patting Worm's neck.

Emperor Song stepped forward.

"You and your dragons have saved us again," he said. "I thank you. And Bo, I will tell your family of your bravery here today."

"Thank you, Emperor. Now I must return to Bracken. The dragons need me," said Bo. "But please tell my family that I will try to come see them soon."

"I will," said the emperor. "And I am sorry for what I have put them through. I will make it up to them."

Bo thanked the emperor. He and Shu both touched Worm.

"Good-bye, Bo," said the emperor. "You have made your kingdom proud."

"Let's go home, Worm," Drake said. They left Emperor Song's kingdom behind them in a flash of green light.

RISE AGAINST MALDRED

econds later, Drake and Bo landed in the Training Room. Rori and Ana rushed over.

"You're okay!" Ana cried.

The boys climbed down from their dragons.

"Yes!" replied Bo. "My family is safe and the emperor is no longer under Maldred's dark spell."

"Shu and Worm were amazing!" Drake said.
"You should have seen them in action!"

Then Drake noticed the worried look on
the girls' faces. "What's wrong?"

"Something has happened to Diego," Rori
said. "Come see."

Drake and Bo followed the girls to Griffith's
workshop. Griffith leaned over Diego, who
was stretched out on a cot.

"Is he asleep?" Drake asked.

"Not exactly," said Griffith. "Diego tried out a new spell — to find Maldred. But it put him into a deep sleep. He has been like this for hours. I am very worried."

Drake and Bo looked at each other.

"Griffith!" cried Bo. "I think we can help. Shu broke the spell that Maldred put on Emperor Song. She has the power to undo magic spells."

Griffith clapped his hands together. "What a wonderful secret power! It may be just what we need to break Diego's spell, too! Can you please ask her to help him?"

Bo nodded and turned to Shu. "Please wash away the spell that is on Diego."

Shu glided right up to Diego. Another misty, blue cloud floated from her mouth. It rained down on Diego. Then he opened his eyes.

"Dragon!" he yelled, sitting up.

"Don't be scared, Diego," said Griffith. "It is only Shu."

"Not Shu," said Diego. "I saw another dragon as I slept."

"What did you see exactly?" Griffith asked Diego.

"Maldred! He had a dragon — an evil dragon with four heads!" Diego said.

"But dragons aren't evil. Are they?" Ana asked.

"Not by nature. But when in the hands of Maldred . . ." Griffith's voice trailed off.

"We should do something," Rori said.

"Yes!" agreed Ana. "We need to find Maldred before he and this four-headed dragon attack the kingdom!"

"Maldred attacked us in Emperor Song's throne room," said Drake. "He sent more red orbs. Lots of them."

"But Worm blasted them all!" added Bo.

Griffith stroked his beard.

"Dragon Masters, you are right," he said. "We cannot risk waiting for Maldred to attack again. We must find him and stop him before it's too late."

"All of us?" Drake asked. "And our dragons, too?"

Griffith nodded. "Yes."

Drake looked at his friends and smiled.

Together, we can face anything! Drake thought.

Griffith turned to the Dragon Masters. "Now, then. It is time for us all to rise against Maldred!"

DRAGON MASTERS
SECRET OF THE WATER DRAGON

Questions and Activities

Look back at the words and pictures to find **CLUES** that something was bothering Bo.

Why does someone want to steal the Dragon Stone?

Look back at the words and pictures to **DESCRIBE** the Raven Guards.

What is Shu the Water Dragon's secret power?

Write a story about what might have happened in Diego's dream.

scholastic.com/branches

TRACEY WEST has written dozens of books for kids. She does her writing in the house she shares with her husband and three stepkids. She also has plenty of animal friends to keep her company. She has two dogs, seven chickens, and one cat, who sits on her desk when she writes! Thankfully, the cat does not weigh as much as a dragon.

GRAHAM HOWELLS lives with his wife and two sons in west Wales, a place full of castles, and legends of wizards and dragons.

Graham has illustrated several books. He has created artwork for film, television, and board games, too. Graham also writes stories for children.

DAMIEN JONES lives with his wife and son in Cornwall — the home of the legend of King Arthur. Cornwall even has its very own castle!

Damien has illustrated children's books. He has also animated films and television programs. He works in a studio surrounded by figures of mystical characters that keep an eye on him as he draws.

DRAGON MASTERS

Read All the Adventures

More
books
coming
soon!

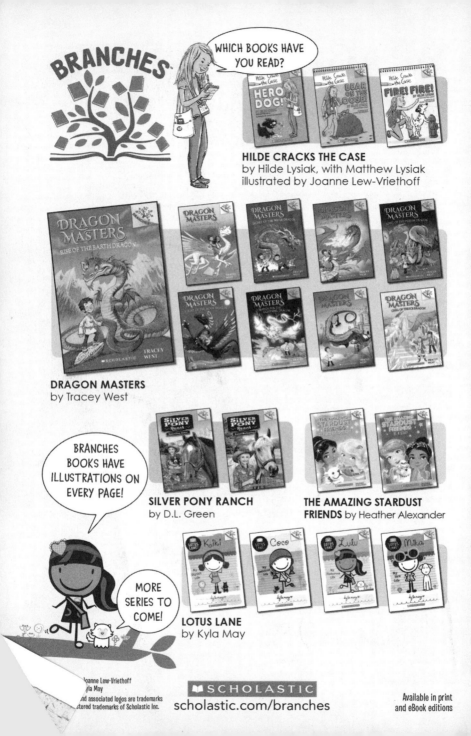